S0-AIH-975

Jamie

Jamie

Charles D. Faulkner, Jr.

Illustrations
By
Robin Faulkner Simunek

Formatting and Text Composition
By
James E. McFarland

iUniverse, Inc.
New York Lincoln Shanghai

Jamie

All Rights Reserved © 2004 by Charles D. Faullkner, Jr.

No part of this book may be reproduced or transmitted in any form or by any means, graphic, electronic, or mechanical, including photocopying, recording, taping, or by any information storage retrieval system, without the written permission of the publisher.

iUniverse, Inc.

For information address:
iUniverse, Inc.
2021 Pine Lake Road, Suite 100
Lincoln, NE 68512
www.iuniverse.com

No part of this book may be used or reproduced in any manner whatsoever without written permission from the author except in the case of brief quotations embodied in critical articles and reviews or in newsletters.

ISBN: 0-595-30251-3

Printed in the United States of America

To all those children
who have watched birds fly,
and wished they too
could fly...just like a bird.

Jamie & Christy

Contents

Jamie's Father

CHAPTER I

Jamie Learns To Fly

This story is about a little brown sparrow named Jamie. I haven't heard anyone tell a story about a sparrow, and that's why I want to tell you about this very special little bird and his adventures.

Jamie was special because he was born at an airport. Most birds don't like to nest and raise their chicks near the runways of busy airports. Trees are hard to find there, and a bird's feathers can be ruffled by the blast from the jet engines as the planes rush by. (Most birds don't like their feathers ruffled.)

Jamie

But Jamie's father was different and daring. He made everyday an adventure. He could fly faster than most sparrows, and he felt a certain kinship with the big, man-made birds that could fly faster and higher than any other bird.

Just for fun, he would swoop down alongside a plane about to take off and race it down the runway. Sometimes he would get too close and would be tossed about in several somersaults as the jet roared ahead. Oh, did his feathers get ruffled! But he didn't mind. When he stopped tumbling, he would fly into the wind, his feathers would smooth out, and he would be just as good as new.

So when he spotted a small shed right next to the runway, he thought, "What a great place for a nest!" On one side, there was a small opening, covered with metal slats and screening. The screening was behind the slats, so it wasn't possible to fly all the way into the shed, but a nest could be built in among the slats. It was a super place because rain wouldn't blow into the nest, and he imagined how much fun it would be to look out at night at the blue and orange lights that were all along the runway. They sort of looked like twinkling Christmas lights, every night!

Jamie's mother, a lovely, slightly plump sparrow, wanted their nest to be built in the hollow of a big statue that stood on the courthouse lawn.

The Nest

She felt such a spot would be just the right place to raise their children, a high and lofty place where they could view the world before them. But she loved Jamie's father, and since he was so excited about building their nest right next to the runway, she tried to be excited, too.

So it came about, as I have mentioned, that Jamie was born in an airport. When he first pecked open his shell and peeked out, a jet roared by. The blast of the exhaust ruffled his tiny, fuzzy, new feathers, and the noise was deafening.

Right then and there he decided, "If that's what it's like outside, I'm staying in my shell."

But that was easier said than done, for the blast had made bigger and longer cracks in his shell and, suddenly, it just fell away.

Jamie thought, "Gee, here I am, whether I want to be or not." As you might imagine, Jamie's parents were excited. Jamie was the first of their brood to hatch. His father wanted to take him right out and teach him how to fly. But Jamie's mother wisely pointed out that it would be best to wait until his wing feathers were fully grown. Jamie felt his parents must love him to be so concerned about him. He began to think life might not be so bad after all, even if the jets did ruffle his feathers.

In a few days, Jamie's sisters hatched. Jamie, being the big brother, was bursting to tell them what life was like. Since he hadn't even been out of the nest, he really didn't know very much about life. But because he was there when his sisters first peeked out of their shells, they thought he had lived a long time and knew a lot of things. So they listened very intently when he told them everything he knew, which wasn't very much.

But, as the days went by, Jamie did learn lots of things. His feathers grew, and he found that with a little hop he could flutter above the nest. Then came the day his father said it was time for Jamie to fly.

Jamie With His Father

Jamie

With a little nudge from his dad, he sailed off into mid-air from his perch on one of the slats. Of course, he didn't sail in any grand manner. In fact, his flight was more like a tailspin. Jamie didn't think he was spinning. He thought the world was spinning! He flapped his wings as fast as he could. Just as the ground was getting very close, he happened to tilt his tail feathers up a bit and he started to fly, skimming the tops of some dandelions growing next to the runway.

Gee, this was great! The world had stopped spinning. The sky was blue. The sun was shining. And it was fun having the dandelions tickle his belly as he flew by!

Jamie's First Flight

It was great until just ahead he saw a small

bush. Now to you or to me, it would be just a

little bush to hop over or run around. But to

9

Jamie

Jamie it looked like a whole forest of twigs, and with thorns, too! He was flying right toward it and he hadn't figured out how to turn. He hadn't even figured out how to stop!

Can you imagine what happened? He was so scared, he shivered right down to his tail feathers. And, do you know what? That did it! His tail feathers moved just a bit, just enough to change his course. He zoomed by the bush, missing a big thorn by the thickness of a feather, which isn't much.

Jamie didn't see how close he came to the thorn because he had shut his eyes. In fact, when he did finally open them, he saw only blue sky.

"How did I miss that bush?" He didn't know. Then he looked down and saw the ground was far below and became frightened again. He was flying higher and higher, and the ground was getting farther and farther away. He was up so high that it was getting cold.

Well, you know how it is when you get cold. You sort of hunch together. Jamie started to hunch. This changed the position of his tail feathers, and he went into a dive.

Down…down…faster and faster. The ground was getting closer and closer!

Jamie thought, "I've got to…to do something. What did I do differently when I was going up? I was flapping my wings. That must be it."

But that wasn't it at all. When he flapped his wings he dove still faster.

He started to panic. "What else can I do—what else can I do?"

Then he remembered he had tail feathers. "I wonder if moving them would make a difference."

He moved them just a little. By arching his back, he started to level out. At first just a little. But then a little bit more and then still more. He was just skimming above the tops of some chimneys and flew right between two workmen who were shingling a roof. They turned to each other and said, "Did you see that crazy bird?"

Then, because Jamie had kept his back arched, he started to climb again. But now he had an idea of what to do. He hunched and went into a dive. Then he arched, buzzed the rooftops, and started to climb. He did this again and again. You might say it was just like a roller coaster ride!

The workmen said, "There's that crazy bird again!" But he wasn't crazy at all—he was flying!

You can imagine that by the time Jamie had learned to set his tail feathers for level flight, as well as for dives and climbs, and had learned to tilt his wings to turn, and had learned to glide to a stop by stretching out his wings and holding them still, and had gotten back to his family's nest, the sun was setting, and he was very tired. But not so tired he couldn't tell everybody everything he had done.

His sisters asked excitedly, "Did you really do that...and that, too?" From time to time his mother sighed, and his father thought, "Boys will be boys." And then, Jamie fell fast asleep, wondering what his father would teach him next.

Jamie and His Family

CHAPTER II

Flying Faster

It wasn't very long after Jamie's first flight that his father was teaching him to race planes down the runway. At first he was just as excited as his father. But Jamie wanted to be able to fly as fast as the jets. It was a bit discouraging to him that, even though he flapped his wings his very hardest, the jet would always pull ahead, going faster and faster, until it was so far ahead that Jamie had to give up the race. Jamie always wondered where the planes were going and what it would be like up so high in the sky.

Jamie

So, one day Jamie decided to try an idea he'd been thinking about. His parents had been hinting it was time he should be leaving the nest, meeting a nice little girl sparrow, and raising a family of his own. Of course Jamie was not interested in girls or raising a family at all. He was interested only in seeing the world—and he had an idea!

So, he circled around a big jet, and just before it started to take off, Jamie swooped down and lighted on top, right behind the cockpit where the pilot and co-pilot sit. What better way to see the world one might say, than to ride piggy-back?

But, as the plane gathered speed, Jamie started to slip. The wind blowing against his little body blew him back and back, faster and faster, right down the length of the plane to its tail. Jamie thought he was going to be blown right off. But just as he thought that, UGH, he backed right into the tail light. And there he was, with one leg and one wing on each side of the tail of the plane, and his tail feathers squashed against the light.

As the plane reached take-off speed, Jamie had to shut his eyes because the wind was blowing so hard. Then, as the plane left the runway and started to climb, he felt one of his feathers pull out. The wind was tugging at every feather on his body!

Jamie thought, "Gee, I'll be naked in another couple of minutes!" Just at that moment, the plane started to bank into a turn. This caused the wind to push at his side, which shoved him right off the plane's tail. Down he went. Head over heels he went!

When he finally got up enough courage to open his eyes, the earth and the sky were all topsy-turvy. He was spinning so fast that he couldn't figure out his position. How could he know how to set his wings or tail feathers? And then, WOOMP!

Jamie fell onto something that was sort of soft. When he opened his eyes, the something was yellow. It was under him and the sky was above, where the sky was supposed to be. He and the thing seemed to be floating through the air. Oh! Oh! Was this Heaven? Was his young life ending?

Falling

Jamie

Then he heard singing! It wasn't the kind of singing he expected to hear in Heaven. He heard a man's voice singing about the sky, the clouds, the mountains, the lakes, the rivers, the trees, the flowers, and all the beauties of nature. How could this be? A floating yellow something up in the sky...and singing...? It didn't make any sense at all.

Jamie was puzzled. He hurt all over and was so tired. He was also afraid that, if he moved, things would go wrong again. But since he could sink, just a little, into this soft thing he was on, he gradually began to feel safe. For a long time he lay very still, just where he had landed.

Finally he mustered enough courage to try moving his right wing. It worked fine. How about that, no broken bones! Then he moved the left wing, then his tail feathers, they worked too. Everything worked, but there was a gap where the feather had blown off.

Jamie wondered what effect that would have on his flying. Very cautiously he stood up and turned around.

All he could see was the sky and clouds and this great big, yellow, ball-like thing that he was standing on. Being the inquisitive sort of fellow that he was, he started walking toward one side. Of course, the farther he walked, the closer he got to the side of this thing. Farther and farther down until, yep, you guessed it!

He started to slide faster and faster right off into mid-air.

Walking

He flapped his wings and though he felt a little stiff, he started to fly. It felt good to fly again, even if he was a little wobbly due to his missing tail feather.

And then he saw what the great big yellow ball thing was. It was a hot air balloon with a wicker basket dangling from ropes. In the basket was a jolly-faced man with a long, bushy beard and a captain's hat. He was singing so merrily that Jamie decided to light on one of the ropes and listen.

You might think that the man would have been rather surprised to see a bird fly in and light on one of the shrouds (as some of the ropes are called). But he just smiled at his little visitor.

Jamie

Flying

The Balloon

It was such a lovely day. The sun was warm,

the sky was blue, the clouds were white, and

all the land below looked so beautiful that it

really didn't seem strange that a sparrow had decided to join him. The jolly-faced man thought, "Why not be friends with all living things?"

So he said, "Hi, sparrow! Decided to hitch a ride, have you? Got tired of flying? Did you think it might be fun to be a passenger on a balloon? I'm captain of this ship. Welcome aboard!"

Jamie began to feel safe, and started to wonder what flying through the air on a balloon will be like.

On The Shrouds

CHAPTER III

Flying With The Wind

Jamie couldn't speak the man's language, but he could tell by his voice that he was friendly. He thought he could almost guess what the man meant when he said, "Welcome aboard," and it gave him a warm feeling down to the very tips of his tail feathers. He wished he could tell the man all he had been through; that he had tried to ride a jet, and that he was very tired, and that he thought the balloon was wonderful.

The balloon was such a bright color, and it sailed through the air so quietly. There was just the right amount of breeze to fluff, but not ruffle, his feathers. He liked it when the basket swayed back and forth—like when he was still in the nest, and the wind rocked it gently.

They sailed along over beautiful green fields where, here and there, a little road would wind; over farm houses and barns, pigs and cows, barking dogs and cackling chickens. Then the ground became more rolling. Up ahead, Jamie could see the white caps of mountains reaching for the sky.

Of course, he didn't know those enormous hills were called mountains, because he had never seen or heard about a mountain before. He just knew they were the biggest, the very biggest hills he had ever seen. Bigger than he thought hills ever grew. (You see he thought hills grew just like birds.)

He had heard about snow falling in winter and he was sure those white caps must be snow. But he wondered, "How can it be winter up at the top of those hills and still be summertime down here?"

Then he remembered! When he was first learning to fly and was climbing higher and higher, it became cooler and cooler, then colder and colder. At that time, he was so frightened he had hardly noticed it. But now he remembered. It must be that if you were high enough, like on top of those hills, it would be winter all the time.

Jamie didn't think he would like that. His mother and father had told him it was much harder to find food in winter and that he should build a nest before it came. Then he'd have time to memorize where seeds had dropped from summer and fall flowers, before the ground was covered with snow. That way he might have a chance of finding them later, if the snow wasn't too deep.

The fluffy white clouds above the balloon were now turning yellow as the sun sank lower in the western sky. Little by little, as it dropped toward the horizon, its rays turned the underside of the clouds into gold. The sky became a darker and darker shade of blue. It was a beautiful display of colors.

Both Jamie and the captain were so thrilled with that symphony of colors, they just stared and stared for a long time. At last the sun finally disappeared below the horizon.

Jamie was the first to turn around to view what other sights might be seen, now that night was coming on.

He was so surprised that he almost fell off his perch. He had forgotten all about the mountains! When Jamie turned, he was looking at a wall of stone. At least that's the way it seemed to him. While they were watching the sunset, they had gotten closer and closer to the mountains. So close, they were now in danger of hitting the stone cliffs.

Jamie chirped as loud as he could, trying to get the captain's attention. He took a good grip of the rope on which he was perched and flapped his wings his very hardest. He tried to help lift the balloon, in order to miss the nearest rocks that were now very close.

When the captain heard all the commotion Jamie was making, he turned around and was just as surprised as Jamie. He jumped so quickly to grab his control levers that his hat was almost jerked off.

Jamie hadn't thought about how a balloon must be lighter than air so it could fly. If it wasn't lighter than air, it would just stay on the ground. In the center, above the basket, the captain had rigged a small stove that would shoot flames out of the top directly into the open bottom of the balloon. The heated air from the flames would then rise into the balloon. It just happens to be a convenient fact that warm air is lighter than cool air. By directing the heated air into the balloon and letting out some of the cooler air through a vent, the balloon could be made to rise higher and higher up into the sky.

Well, as I said, the captain grabbed his control levers. They had just missed the nearest rock by inches, and the balloon was sailing through a crevice. The side of the mountain towered way above them on each side and the branches of trees that had grown on small rocky ledges seemed to be reaching out for them just ahead.

Jamie thought that maybe, if he tugged on the ropes on the other side of the basket, the nearest tree might not be able to reach them. But, as he jumped for the ropes, the flames leaped from the stove! The force of that heated air just above the flames drove Jamie right up, into the middle of the balloon, head over heels. Ooh, was that air hot!

The force of the hot air rising from the flames kept Jamie tumbling in mid-air, right in the center of the balloon. He was like a ball that a seal bounces off its nose. One minute Jamie would seem to be falling. Then, the hot air would carry him higher. All this was happening so fast that he couldn't even think. From one moment to the next, he couldn't decide if he was right side up or upside-down. If he'd had time to think and had been a boy or girl (which of course he wasn't, since he was a bird), he probably would have thought that this must be how a toy yo-yo feels.

Jamie

Tumbling

With the first blast of the flames the balloon had started to rise—just a little at first, but then a bit more, and then some more. It was just enough to miss most of the nearest tree. But several of the smallest branches scraped across the basket and some of the ropes, catching here and there. These twigs caught hold just for a second, before breaking, and then the balloon was free again.

Since the balloon was sailing through the crevice very fast, the branches, catching on the basket and ropes caused the entire balloon to spin like a top. Jamie was tumbling about so much inside that he didn't notice the spinning. But for the captain, it was a different story.

Have you ever thought what it would be like to be small enough to be able to hang onto a top while it is spinning? Well, that's what it was like for the captain.

Jamie

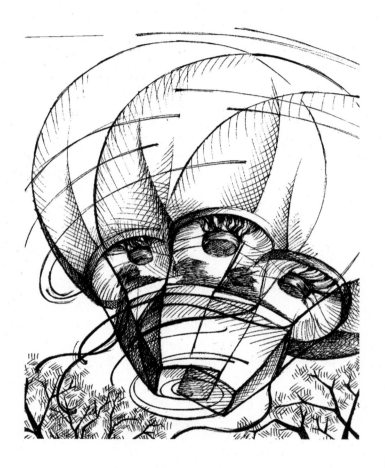

Spinning

All of a sudden almost everything swirled
around him. To the captain the cliffs, the
crevice, the sky, all became a big blur. He felt

dizzier and dizzier. He could only lean on the side of the basket and hold onto two of the ropes.

The lever that makes the flames shoot out of the stove had been pushed to "full open" by the captain, causing flames to roar up. As the balloon was spinning, it was also rising. Lucky that it was, for the crevice was getting narrower and narrower! They reached the top of the crevice just before it became a little slit high up on the side of the mountain.

But now, being above the sheltering sides of the crevice, the wind, racing up the mountainside, carried them even faster over the jagged rocks at the very top.

Have you ever noticed how smoke will swirl out of a chimney when the wind is blowing?

Jamie

Though you can't see it, the wind always swirls after it has blown across a chimney or the top of a mountain. Just as soon as the balloon cleared the mountaintop it was caught up in the swirling air currents.

Now besides spinning, the balloon and basket began to tip, first this way and then that. The basket swung around so far that it almost dumped the poor captain out.

When this happened, the flames and hot air shot along the side of the opening rather than directly into the center of the balloon. Jamie stopped tumbling. He fell flat against the inside of the balloon, his wings and legs stretched out at different angles. Then, as the balloon began to swing back to an upright position, he started to slide down toward the opening!

As the balloon continued its swing, Jamie fell right through the opening. He just missed the flames, went through the ropes and was tossed out into space!

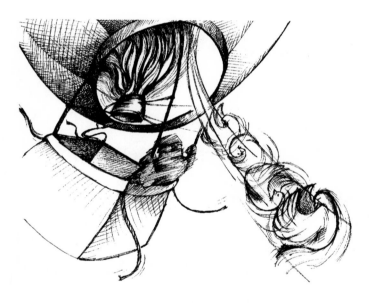

Falling Out

The swirling wind caught Jamie and took him on what the captain would have said was like a super roller-coaster ride. Up and around, down and under, into a spiral, back up again (just missing the top of a tree), then shoot-the-shoots, skimming above the rocks, down the side of the mountain and into a lovely valley he fell!

Of course Jamie didn't know it was a lovely valley because he had shut his eyes just as tightly as he could. He thought every moment would be his last. And when he finally came crashing through the branches of a big maple tree he thought it WAS his last!

Fortunately for Jamie the top-most branches had new twigs that bent easily so they helped cushion the shock as he fell through, slipping across a leaf here, bouncing off a branch there, losing a couple of feathers, just missing a nest of sparrows that shrieked as he passed, and finally landing on some leaves in a bushel basket that had been left under the tree. He was too exhausted and frightened to move. But, at least, he was not on the ground!

You probably know that the ground is a dangerous place for a bird like Jamie. Even dogs that are wonderful pets might pick up an injured bird, sometimes just to bring it to their master. Because their teeth are sharp and their jaws are strong, they might kill a small bird without meaning to. Jamie's only chance for survival was in not being noticed. He needed time to rest and regain his strength.

Jamie

The Maple Tree

Autumn was just coming in the valley, and
if you've ever seen maple trees in the early

autumn you know their large leaves turn the most beautiful shades of yellow and red at that time of year.

I like to think that all living things are aware of what is happening around them, even trees. Whether the maple tree was aware of Jamie's plight, I cannot say. But, just as soon as he landed in the basket, he was covered by a blanket of leaves. What a pretty cover it was! Maybe the wind caused all those yellow and red leaves to fall. Maybe Jamie knocked them loose by bumping into so many branches. Or, just possibly, the tree had something to do with it. We'll never know for sure.

It was warm and cozy under the leaves. The cool air of the night didn't reach him. Of course, he shivered from fear once or twice when he thought about all the things that had happened to him, but gradually his fear gave way to sleep, and he slept for a very long time. As he slept, he dreamed that he would wake up to a whole new world.

Under The Leaves

CHAPTER IV

Christy

At wasn't until late the next morning that he woke up. Every muscle ached. Even his eyelids hurt from being held shut for so long.

First he tried turning his head. Everything seemed to work all right there. His right wing seemed to move as it should, his left one too, and both legs. He gave a sigh of relief and made a promise to himself to fly only by his own power in the future. He decided he would take a deep breath, get up on his feet, and fly up into the tree where he would be safer. Then, he would decide what to do next.

It didn't quite work out that way. He finally did get to his feet on the third try. But when he flapped his wings, nothing happened. He picked up his right foot and then his left, to make sure they weren't stuck in the leaves.

Then he looked at his wings. No wonder he couldn't fly. Some of his feathers were gone. What a sorry-looking sight! What a sad little bird! What would he do? How could he get food? How could he stay hidden long enough for new feathers to grow?

All the while the sparrows in the nest above were watching his every move. Christina, a little girl sparrow about the same age as Jamie, leaned over the nest so far she slipped off, but then flew down and lighted in the bushel basket just by his side.

Jamie hadn't noticed this and, with a sigh, tried to wiggle back under the leaves, though not very successfully. Then he heard, or thought he heard, "Hello."

He turned his head and looked into what he thought were the most beautiful eyes he had ever seen.

Christina cocked her head and said, "What on earth happened? Why did you fall out of the sky? We heard the crash and saw you bounce through the branches. You only missed our nest by inches. Did you hear me scream? I wanted to fly down to see how you were, but mother said I would only add to the commotion and might put you in greater danger. So, I had to wait until now, when I sort of accidentally slid out of our nest. Are you all

right? Can you talk? You look so funny without all your feathers!"

Jamie and Christy

At first Jamie didn't say a word. In fact he
hadn't heard most of the questions. He wasn't
thinking about the questions. He was thinking
that she was the most beautiful sparrow he
had ever seen. Her feathers looked so soft,

their colors were so delicate, and her voice sounded so sweet.

Her voice? It had just said, "You look so funny without all of your feathers."

Jamie tried to say something, but all he could manage was a very weak, "Hello."

"You poor dear! You must have had a terrible experience. You just rest here. I'll cover you with leaves and then get you some water and food."

Those words sounded like the most beautiful music he'd ever heard. As she placed the last leaf over him he shut his eyes and thought about what a nice, kind sparrow she was. In a few minutes she was back with a wet leaf she had plucked out of a nearby stream.

A Drop of Water

He was able to suck off one or two drops of water. Then she was back again with a seed— then another and another. They tasted so good!

It took a while for Jamie's feathers to grow enough for him to fly again. All during this time, Christina, as her parents had named her (but she liked to be called "Christy"), brought Jamie water and seeds and covered him with leaves. Whenever she was quite sure there were no animals or other birds nearby that might harm Jamie, she again asked him all her questions.

He answered them one by one, and told her about his adventures. Christy told him she thought he was very brave. She also thought he had been rather foolish, but she didn't tell him that. She told him she had always lived in the valley with her parents in their nest in the branches above, but now she would like to raise a family. She said she had spotted a lovely place to build a nest. A house farther down in the valley had an opening up near the peak of the roof with some slats and they were spaced just right so she could squeeze in. A nest would be safe, warm, and dry inside.

Jamie of course knew all about openings with slats and had to agree that it would be an ideal spot for a nest. The valley would indeed be a lovely place to live. Then Christy said that someday, if she and Jamie had children, they would be so excited to hear him tell of his jet and balloon trips. Suddenly, Jamie found the idea of raising a family to be a pleasant one.

At last, Jamie was able to flutter a bit. Then he was able to fly up a short distance and grab hold of the bark on the trunk of the tree, then he reached the lowest branch. After that, in a day or two, he was really flying again.

Finally, just before the first snow, Jamie and Christy completed their nest behind the slats.

As I am coming to the end of this story, spring has arrived, and I can hear the chirping of more than just two sparrows in the nest.

I suppose you are wondering how it happens that I know so much about Jamie. Well, all I can say is that my house has a slatted opening near the peak of the roof, and that "a little bird told me."

The End

POSTLUDE

To my dear grandchildren,
Michael, Lisa, and Kathleen,
who are always an inspiration.
May each of your flights through
life be rich in fulfillment.

0-595-30251-3